Police Nan and Spike the Cat-Detective

The Mystery of the Toyshop Robber

Written by Dawn McNiff

Illustrated by Andy Catling

Collins

Chapter 1

I woke up from a lovely dream about fish cakes.
I purred, stretched out my paws and yawned. I started
to wash my tail but stopped mid-lick.

Nan was putting on her old police helmet. Uh oh …
What was she up to *now*?

"Come on, Spike!" she called. Her eyes glittered as she
pulled on her best cardigan. "I just heard on the TV
– someone keeps robbing Madame Jouette's Toyshop
at night. It's a big MYSTERY because no one knows
how the robber gets in! It's definitely a case for Police
Nan and cat-detective Spike to the rescue."

Oh no! I jumped off my comfy cushion with a scowl.
Not again.

Honestly, Nan was supposed to be retired from
the police, but she would NOT stop.

And yes, I *was* good at catching robbers. I used to be
a cat burglar, so I know lots of tricks.

But when Nan rescued me from the cats' home,
I turned my tail on crime.

Now I was a goodie, I just wanted to stay indoors, and cat-nap all day.

But I could *never* let Nan go and solve crimes by herself – she always got in a muddle and then in LOTS of trouble. Last time, she lost her glasses and arrested a scarecrow.

Nan was looking everywhere for her handbag. It was behind a cushion, so I pointed to it with my paw.

"Oh, well done, Spikey. Whatever would I do without you?" said Nan, slurping the last of her coffee. "I've phoned Madame Jouette and told her we're on our way, so let's go!"

I sighed and jumped inside the handbag. I curled up at the bottom next to her purse, knitting and bag of chocolate.

I wondered where we were going *this* time. I hoped Madame Jouette's Toyshop wasn't too far away. Once, we had to go to Spain to solve a crime. Another time, we even went to *Australia* and I had to save Nan from a big kangaroo.

"Drat this silly rain," said Nan, as we went out of the door. "We'd better take the bus to the airport."

To the *airport*? Oh no …

"We'll catch that naughty toyshop robber, Spike," Nan whispered breathlessly, as she bustled to the bus stop under her umbrella.

It was a bumpy ride inside her handbag and I had
to cling on with my claws.

"Ooh, isn't it exciting!" Nan squealed. "A top-secret,
detective mission to PARIS. Look out, France – here
we come!"

Chapter 2

I had to use my cat-burglar powers of disguise to sneak on to the plane with Nan. I stayed very still and pretended to be Nan's furry cushion, and no one noticed me.

It was only when we were on the plane that I realised she was still wearing her fluffy slippers.

I clawed her toe to tell her.

"Oops," she tutted. "Silly me! But never mind. Maybe slippers are fashionable in Paris!"

I rolled my eyes.

We took a taxi through Paris to the toyshop.

The shop was in a huge, old building, piled high
with every kind of toy – dolls, balls, cars, fairy wings,
animal costumes, kites, robots and paints.

A lady in a posh dress greeted us.

"Are you Police Nan and Spike?" the lady said in a French accent. She looked down at Nan's slippers in surprise. "*Bonjour*! I'm Madame Jouette and that's Peter, my dear grandson. He arrived from England recently to live with me."

She pointed to a small boy with big, round glasses in the book corner. He didn't say hello, but just blushed and hid behind his book.

"Peter and I are so glad you're here," cried Madame Jouette. "The robber breaks in each night, even though all the doors and windows are locked. We live just next door, but we never hear a thing. We can't imagine how he gets in." Madame Jouette dabbed her eyes with a tissue. "And even stranger – the robber steals our best-selling toys, but he brings them back after a week!"

"Goodness me! How very odd," said Nan. "Well, don't worry. We'll stay in the shop tonight and catch him!"

"Ooh-la-la – you're so *brave*," said Madame Jouette. "Well, good night and good luck!"

Chapter 3

The shop closed for the night, and all the customers and staff went home. As the sun went down, the shop grew darker. The moon was behind a cloud, so the shop was only lit by tiny stars twinkling through the window.

Nan turned on her torch, so she could see.

"So, Spikey," she whispered, pouring cream into a toy boat for my dinner. "This is a clever robber, so we need a clever trick to catch him. What do you think?"

I licked the cream off my chin and climbed up on
some high shelves for a birds-eye view of the shop.
I stared through the darkness – cats can see in
the dark much better than humans.

I spotted some pots of playdough. Yes! Now I had
an idea.

I jumped down and knocked the playdough on to
the floor. I rolled across the soft dough to make it flat.

Nan watched me.

"Ah, I see your idea, Spike!" she said. "If the robber
runs away, he'll leave footprints on the playdough
and we'll have clues. Then we can work out where
he's getting in."

Nan laid out the flattened playdough on the floor.

Then we hid in the shadows on a beanbag and waited.

I snuggled up on Nan's lap, purring.

The moon came out from behind a cloud and filled the shop with a pale, silver light.

"I'm just resting my eyes for a minute," said Nan. "But I'm definitely still awake."

Then she fell fast asleep.

I sighed. Now it was only me on guard.

Oh, what was that noise?

Was it just a bird on the roof?

I jumped off Nan's lap and slunk behind
some dolls. I peered out across the dark shop,
my whiskers quivering.

I heard soft footsteps.

Then I saw the shadowy shape of the robber. Under his
arm, he was carrying something shiny that glinted in
the moonlight. He was stealing a toy!

I crouched down, ready to pounce.

But then … oh!

Nan snored. A very long, LOUD snore.

It made me jump. I flew into the air, knocking some pots of slime off a shelf.

SPLAT! The gooey slime went all over the floor.

The robber heard the crash and dashed away.

He ran past the fancy-dress area, and I glimpsed his reflection in a mirror which was lit up by the moon. He had massive, round eyes – and he looked sort of *furry*.

Then he seemed to vanish behind all the teddies.

Nan woke up and leapt to her feet.

"Oh, quick, Spike!" she cried "It's the robber!"

I rolled my eyes. She was way too late.

She tried to run after the robber, but she'd forgotten
she was wearing her fluffy slippers. She tripped over
her own feet, slipped on the slime and fell flat on
her face.

"Oof!" she cried. She staggered up, covered
in slime. "Don't worry, Spikey, I'm not hurt.
But the robber escaped."

I sighed.

She shone her torch across the shop.

"But he left that behind!" she said, aiming the torch beam at a glow-in-the-dark football. "And look – he left footprints in the playdough!"

I rushed over to look.

No, they weren't footprints – they were *paw prints*.

So, the robber was furry. He had big, round eyes. And he had paws.

Was the robber an *animal*?

Chapter 4

In the morning, I searched and sniffed near
the teddies where the robber had vanished.
I could definitely smell him, but there were no
windows and doors nearby. *How* had he got out?

Madame Jouette was talking to Nan. "It's terrible,"
she wailed. "The robber stole a dog-robot – another
best-selling toy."

Ah, a robot! That was the shiny, metal thing under
the robber's arm.

"But he brought back this glow-in-the-dark football
which he stole last week," sniffed Madame Jouette.
"It's muddy, so it's been played with. Very bizarre."

"Don't worry," said Nan, giving her a tissue.
"We'll catch him tonight."

25

When the shop closed, I led Nan over to the teddies and pointed with my paw to show her where we should wait for the robber.

"Good, Spikey," said Nan. "Now this is my plan. The robber moves very fast, so I'm going to wear these roller-skates, so I can catch up with him. And I'm going to knit a huge net, so we can throw it over him. Isn't that brilliant!"

I sighed. Nan's plan sounded like trouble to me. But she was already strapping on the roller-skates and getting out her knitting needles.

I needed to think of a better trick to catch the robber.

I searched the shop for ideas and then I thought of it – glue! I clawed some holes in a tube of glitter glue. I squashed it with my paws until glue squirted out all over the floor.

"Yes, Spikey – that's a good trap," cried Nan, clapping her hands. "The robber will get glued to the floor and I can skate over and catch him with my net – easy-peasy! We are a top team."

We hid amongst the teddies to wait.

Nan turned on her torch, adjusted her glasses and started knitting a net.

Click, click, click … The noise of her knitting needles made me dozy.

I purred, padding the soft teddies with my paws – it reminded me of being a kitten with my cat mum.

My eyes drooped.

Suddenly, I woke with a start.

There was a loud, creaking noise. A trap door was opening in the floor next to us.

All the teddies slid backwards and the robber crept out.

So that's how he was getting in!

"STOP, thief!" Nan cried, leaping to her feet and wobbling on her skates.

The robber ran. Nan skated after him.

"I'll catch you this time," shouted Nan. "YOU'RE UNDER ARREST!"

But her glasses fell off her nose.

She swerved and skated over the glue.

"Ahhhh – help!" she cried.

The wheels on her skates stuck to the floor and stopped spinning. The wheel axles snapped and the wheels broke off.

Nan tumbled and landed on top of the teddies and her knitting.

"Help, Spike – I'm caught in my own net!" she cried.

I scampered over to help her. But Nan was wriggling so much that I got tangled up in the knitting too.

And before I could get free, a big, furry arm grabbed me. It pulled me and Nan's ball of wool down into the trap door.

"MiaOW!" I cried, as we slid down a tunnel.

Was the robber stealing ME? Did he think I was a soft toy?

Chapter 5

Down, down, down, we went.

The robber was holding me tight in his arms.

I stayed still and pretended to be a toy cat to trick him.
When he squashed my tummy, I squeaked like a toy.

BUMP!

We'd landed in an old cellar. It was lit by small
candles which made a flickering, orange glow in
the dark.

The robber dropped me on the floor. I thought he was a furry animal, but now in the dim light, I could see he was wearing a bear costume.

My back arched, my tail bristled and my claws were out.

With a hiss, I did a big leap and pounced on the robber. He rolled on to the floor. I stood on top of him, so he couldn't escape.

The robber squealed and pulled off his bear hat. Underneath, he was just a small boy. The massive, round eyes were just his glasses.

And then I saw … the robber was Madame Jouette's grandson, Peter!

"Oh, but you're not a toy!" he cried. "You're Spike the cat-detective." He burst into tears. "And now you think I'm an awful robber."

There was a big clatter and a whooshing noise behind us.

"Stop – thief!" someone shouted from the tunnel.

PLOP!

Nan slid out headfirst and landed in a heap on the floor.

"I'm here, Spikey," Nan puffed. "I followed the thread of wool and found you."

Oh! Now I saw that Nan's knitting wool was still wound around my tail.

"And good boy – it looks like you've already caught the robber." Nan staggered up and peered at Peter in surprise.

"*You're* the robber?" she said.

"Oh no," said Peter, hanging his head. "I'm in such big trouble."

"Ah, I see!" said Nan, looking around the cellar. "You used an old tunnel from your house into the shop! But why did you steal the toys?"

"To make friends," Peter sobbed. "When I got here from England, I didn't have any friends. I thought the children in our street might want to play with me if I brought them toys."

"Oh dear," said Nan, handing him a tissue.

"I'm sorry!" he sniffed. "I always brought the toys back, so I thought it wasn't really stealing, because I was only borrowing them. But I know it was wrong."

"There, there," said Nan. She dug into her pocket.
"Here you are – have some chocolate. That usually
cheers me up if I'm down in the dumps."

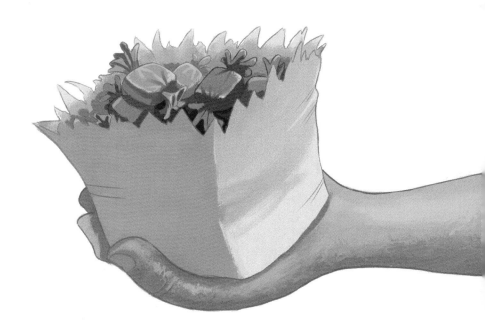

"Grandma Jouette will be so cross with me," sniffed
Peter, with a mouthful of chocolate.

"No, you must say sorry and we'll help you explain,"
said Nan kindly. "And do you know what? I bet your
friends like *you*, not your toys. Because you're very
nice, you know."

"Do you think?" said Peter. And he gave Nan
a big hug, while I rubbed around his legs, purring.

Chapter 6

The next morning, the sun came up and flooded the toyshop with warm sunlight.

Nan had a long conversation with Madame Jouette over a cup of coffee and explained everything. Now Madame Jouette was all smiles.

"Well, it's been very surprising," she said. "But I'm glad the mystery is solved. Peter is sorry that he took the toys. And I'm sorry that I didn't know he needed more friends. But just look at him now."

We all stared out of the window.

Peter was in the street below, playing tag with some children. He waved up at us with a big grin.

"There, I was right," said Nan. "His friends *do* like him, not just the toys."

"Oh, my darling Peter," said Madame Jouette, dabbing her eyes. "And this has given me an idea – I've decided to start a toy library for the local children. They can borrow toys ... without coming through a tunnel!"

"How lovely, dear," said Nan.

It was a happy ending, but now I was tired. I clawed Nan's jeans, yawning.

"Yes, Spikey," said Nan. "Our work is done. It's home time."

We said our goodbyes.

It wasn't long before I was snuggled on Nan's lap on the plane.

"Well done, my boy," whispered Nan, stroking me. "Another crime solved."

I fell asleep, purring and dreaming of my cosy cushion and fish cakes for my dinner.

Ways to catch a robber

playdough for footprints

roller-skates for fast chases

a knitted net

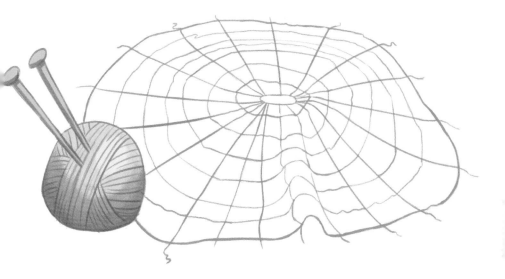

a glue trap

Ideas for reading

Written by Christine Whitney
Primary Literacy Consultant

Reading objectives:
- discuss the sequence of events in books
- make inferences on the basis of what is being said and done
- answer and ask questions
- predict what might happen on the basis of what has been read so far

Spoken language objectives:
- ask relevant questions to extend their understanding and knowledge

- use spoken language to develop understanding through speculating, hypothesising, imagining and exploring ideas
- participate in discussions, role play and improvisations

Curriculum links: PSHE – health and well-being, making friends; Science – everyday materials

Word count: 2519

Interest words: detective, mission, mystery, arrest

Resources: exercise book and pencils

Build a context for reading

- Check children's understanding of the word *mystery*. Ask them if they have ever been involved in a mystery before at home or at school.
- Look at the title and the image on the front cover. Ask children to explain what is happening to Police Nan and what mystery she has to solve. How do they think that Spike will help her?
- Read the blurb together. Ask children to predict what the *terrible muddles* might be and how Spike might *keep Nan out of trouble*.

Understand and apply reading strategies

- Read Chapter 1 together, pausing at the end of page 6. Ask children what clues there are as to where Nan and Spike are going this time.